Toy Story 4 is the next chapter in
Disney • Pixar's Toy Story series. The film sees
Woody and Buzz Lightyear on yet another exciting
adventure where their worlds are turned upside
down by the arrival of a new toy.

Autumn
Publishing

Published in 2019
by Autumn Publishing
Cottage Farm
Sywell
NN6 0BJ
www.igloobooks.com

Autumn is an imprint of Bonnier Books UK

LEO002 0319
2 4 6 8 10 9 7 5 3 1
ISBN 978-1-78905-535-1

Printed and manufactured in China

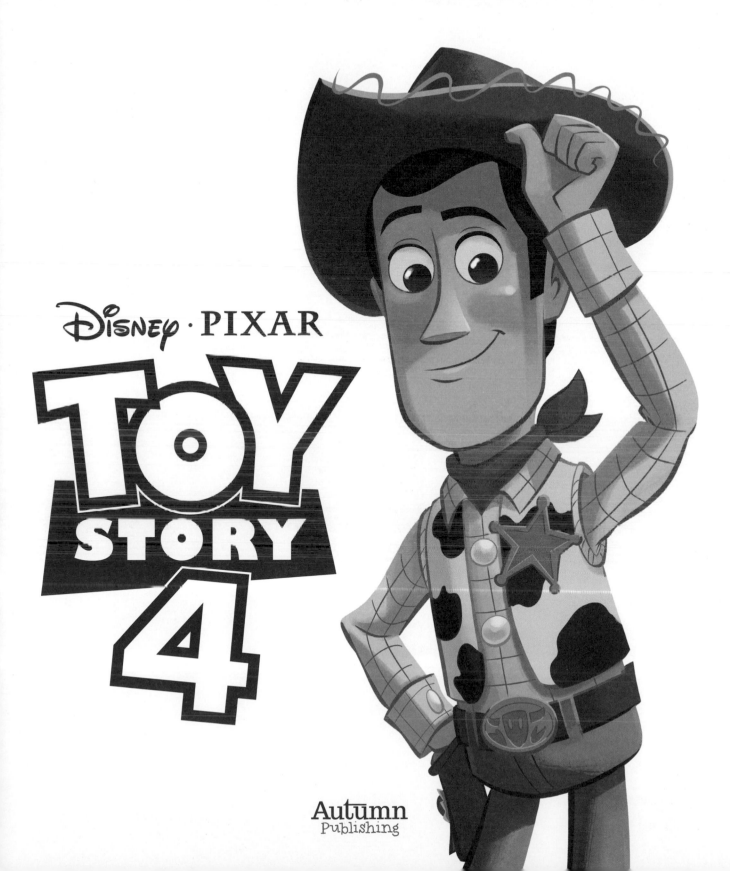

Now that Andy is at college, Woody
has had to adjust to life with a new kid.
But the arrival of a troublesome new
toy leads the cowboy on an exciting
adventure with old friends and new.

Buzz has taken the move to Bonnie's room in his stride. He is as trustworthy as ever and always ready for a new adventure. All his friends know Buzz would go to infinity and beyond to help them.

Confident and loyal, Jessie has come
on in leaps and bounds since Andy took
her into his toy collection. Now owned by
Bonnie, she has become one of the little
girl's most played with toys.

Bo is as brave and tough as they come.
Since she was last with Woody and the gang,
she has been on lots of adventures. Now living
a new life as a lost toy, Bo teams up with
Woody to rescue a toy named Forky.

Forky is learning what it means to be a toy. Created at preschool from art supplies, the spork doesn't quite understand the rules of being a toy, which leaves Woody with a very big problem.

Duke has the swagger of Canada's greatest
stuntman, but he hasn't been the same since
his last kid got rid of him. His TV advert showed
him jumping a long way, yet Duke has never
been able to match that in real life.

Ducky and Bunny are two toys
who are literally inseparable, as they're
attached by their wing and paw. They have
spent years as carnival game prizes,
waiting to be won by a kid.

Talking doll Gabby Gabby is a
popular toy from the 1950s, but not
all toys are perfect straight out of the box.
After spending years in display cabinets,
Gabby Gabby just wants a kid.

She may be small in size, but
Pet Patrol Officer Giggle McDimples
is a seasoned law enforcement officer. As
well as being spirited and funny, she is
one of the most gifted detectives
you will ever meet.

Bonnie is the young girl who Andy
passed his toys on to. She is imaginative
and shy. Though she has given them a good
home, there are some toys she plays with
more than others. She especially likes
Forky, who she made at preschool.

One night, when a storm was raging outside, there was an emergency.
A toy had been left outside. Woody hurried into Molly's room. Andy's
sister's bedroom had a window with a view of the whole front garden.

With Bo Peep's help, Woody climbed onto the nightstand. When they
looked outside, a sudden flash of lightning revealed RC! He was stuck
in the mud by the driveway.

All the toys helped to open
the window. Woody held
onto Slinky Dog as he leapt
outside to the ground.

Everyone worked together
and, at last, Woody pulled
RC out of the mud!

Slinky's spring pulled them
back to the bedroom window
just as a stranger's car pulled
into the driveway.

Woody finished getting everyone through the window when – WHAM – it was slammed shut. Woody looked through the glass. Andy's mum was putting Bo and her sheep into a box! Molly didn't want them anymore, so the stranger had come to take Bo away to a new kid.

Bo wanted Woody to come with her. But at that moment, Woody heard Andy looking for him – he knew he couldn't leave his kid. Bo wiped a raindrop from Woody's cheek and settled back into the box. Woody watched as the man loaded the box into his car and drove away.

Years later, Andy outgrew his toys and gave them to an imaginative little girl named Bonnie. She loved playing with Woody and the rest of Andy's toys.

But Bonnie also had toys of her own and, as time went on, Woody found himself being played with less and less. He spent most of his time sharing a dark wardrobe with Bonnie's baby toys.

Then, one day, it was Bonnie's induction at preschool. Wanting to make sure she was okay, Woody hid himself in her bag and went with her.

The children were making pencil holders at the induction. Bonnie was getting ready to start when a kid took her art supplies and accidentally threw some of them in the bin. Bonnie's eyes filled with tears.

Woody climbed out of the backpack, sneaked to the bin and took out as many items as he could carry. To distract Bonnie, he threw a box of crayons on the floor and then took everything else to Bonnie's table.

Bonnie felt much better when she saw the supplies. She picked up a spork and glued a pair of eyes onto it.

Bonnie added arms, legs and even wrote her name on her project's stick feet. She decided to name him Forky. Bonnie's teacher was impressed and the little girl smiled. Woody was relieved to see her happy.

At the end of the induction, Bonnie put Forky into her backpack, right next to Woody. Then suddenly, Forky came to life!

Later, back home in Bonnie's room, Woody told the toys that Bonnie had made a new friend at preschool. "Everyone," said Woody, "I want you to meet… Forky!"

Woody explained that Forky was important to Bonnie. They had to make sure nothing bad happened to him.

Woody soon discovered that it wasn't easy looking after
Forky. The spork constantly ran to the bin because it was
where he felt safest.

With Bonnie's family deciding to take a road trip
in their campervan before the start of the school
year, Woody knew he'd have to be extra careful
to make sure Forky stayed safe.

Forky was a handful. At every stop, he tried
to run to the nearest rubbish bin. Each time,
Woody chased after him and brought him
back before Bonnie noticed.

When night fell, Forky climbed
up towards an open window.
"I am not a toy," he declared.
"I'm a spork."

And with that, Forky jumped
out of the moving campervan.
"Freedom!"

Woody gasped. He knew he had
to go after him. He told the toys
he would meet them at the RV
park.

Then, the cowboy leapt out of
the window to follow Forky.

Woody called out for Forky.
He soon found the spork by
the side of the road and began
dragging him towards the
RV park.

On the way, Woody explained
that Bonnie loved Forky the
same way Forky loved trash.

"Oh Woody, I get it now," said
Forky. "I am Bonnie's trash!"
The spork broke into a run. He
needed to get back to Bonnie!

The two toys reached the town of Grand Basin just before morning. As they approached the RV park, Woody saw something in the window of a shop called Second Chance Antiques.

The cowboy gasped. It was Bo Peep's lamp! Forky wanted to keep moving,
but Woody had to see if Bo was in the shop.

Woody and Forky called out for Bo, but they saw no sign of her.
As they turned to leave, they were spotted by a doll named Gabby Gabby
and a ventriloquist's dummy named Benson. She asked Woody if he was lost.

"Lost? No, no, but we are looking for a lost toy," Woody replied.

Gabby Gabby said she knew Bo and would take them to her.

Gabby Gabby noticed the pullstring in
Woody's back and began to ask him about
his voice box.
She explained that her record was perfect,
but her voice box was broken. She needed a
new one so she could be complete – and Woody's
voice box would be a perfect fit.

Woody felt nervous. He turned
to Forky. "We gotta go."

"You can't leave," Gabby Gabby said.
"You have what I need."

Suddenly, more dummies surrounded the pram! Woody grabbed Forky and sprinted down the aisle. But the dummies were quick – they wrenched Forky from Woody's grasp. Without any other options, Woody pulled his string. Harmony, the shop owner's granddaughter, heard Woody and picked him up on her way to the park. Forky was left behind with the dummies.

Once Harmony was distracted, Woody made a run for it. But a bus full of children overran the playground. It was mayhem! Woody dodged and hid from the kids so he could return to the shop for Forky.

As Woody sneaked away, he saw a small sheep run by. He turned to get a closer look and noticed a girl playing with a toy. The girl picked up the cowboy and introduced him to her other toy – it was Bo Peep!

Once the girl put them down and left,
Woody and Bo escaped into the nearby
bushes. They were thrilled to see each
other. Just then, a vehicle disguised as
a skunk skidded to a stop. Bo's sheep,
Billy, Goat and Gruff, jumped out of
the vehicle and tackled Woody.
"Hold on there!" laughed Woody.
"I missed you, too!"

Bo told Woody she'd been a lost toy
for seven years. One of her closest
friends was a tiny police officer named
Giggle McDimples.

Woody said he needed help to rescue
Forky from Gabby Gabby and bring
him back to Bonnie.

Back at the antique shop, Gabby Gabby sat with Forky in her glass cabinet. Suddenly, Harmony returned to the shop. Gabby Gabby watched in wonder as the little girl pulled out her tea set and mimicked every move Harmony made.

She wanted nothing more in the world than to make Harmony her kid. Only one thing stood in her way – her broken voice box. She asked Forky to tell her everything he knew about Woody.

Meanwhile, Buzz had left the RV park to go looking for Woody. Unfortunately, he'd been found by a carnival worker and was now the top prize at the Star Adventurer game! This upset two stuffed toys called Ducky and Bunny.

Ducky started kicking at Buzz's head while Bunny swung him. Buzz closed his helmet right on Ducky's foot and pulled himself out of the plastic tie that held him in place. The three toys struggled and fell to the ground in a heap!

Now he was free, Buzz quickly resumed his search for Woody. Ducky and Bunny chased after him as they felt Buzz owed them a kid.

It wasn't long before Buzz, Ducky and Bunny found Woody, along with Bo, the sheep and Giggle McDimples on the roof of the antique shop. Woody explained what happened and that they were on their way to rescue Forky.

Back at the campervan, Bonnie's family were ready to leave. Woody, Buzz and Forky would be left behind! Jessie had an idea. She jumped out of the window and made her way to the front of the vehicle. Then, there was a loud noise – POP! Jessie had popped the tyre and bought them more time.

Inside the shop, Bo led the toys to
a gap in the shelves and pointed
to Gabby Gabby's glass cabinet.
"That's most likely where your
Forky is being kept," said Bo.

It seemed impossible to get across
without being seen by the dummies
or the shop cat, Dragon. Bo had
a plan.

But Woody didn't stick to Bo's plan
and ran towards the cabinet.

Suddenly, a dummy grabbed
Woody. To protect their friend,
Bo's sheep bit onto the dummy's
trousers. The dummy ran off, with
the sheep still attached to him.
Bo was upset. Now her sheep
were missing, too! They needed
a new plan.

Bo took Woody to meet Duke Caboom, Canada's greatest stuntman.
She told him that they needed his help rescuing her sheep and Forky.
He had to jump across the aisle on his motorcycle.

"No!" exclaimed Duke. "Nope. Nuh-uh. No way!"

He hadn't attempted a jump in years and wanted no part in Bo's plan.

Woody told Duke that he needed to rescue Forky for his kid. Duke began to think about his own kid, Rejean. When Duke couldn't jump like the toy in the TV advert, Rejean threw him away. Duke began to wail at the memory of his kid.

Bo convinced the stunt man to believe in himself even if it meant jumping and crashing. Duke felt his confidence return. He would do the jump!

As the toys moved towards Gabby Gabby's cabinet Woody told Bo that he was impressed by her skills. "You've handled this lost toy life better than I could," he said.

"You're selling yourself short," replied Bo. "I think you'd make a great lost toy."

Soon after, with the help of Duke's jump, Bo rescued her sheep, but
Woody's attempt to rescue Forky went wrong and the cowboy ended
up on top of Dragon. The cat was not happy about his new passenger.

In the meantime, the rest of the toys had fallen to the floor. Bo told
everyone to grab onto a ribbon that was attached to Woody.

Duke zoomed past Dragon and the cat chased Duke through the shop!
As they left, Woody saw the dummies pick up Forky.
He had been left behind.

Duke led Dragon through a cat flap and into the back alley. After the cat ran off, the toys checked to make sure everyone was okay.

Woody insisted that they go back for Forky because Bonnie needed him. "No. You need Bonnie," said Bo. "There's plenty of kids out there. It can't just be about the one you're still clinging to."

The toys followed Bo – no one wanted to return to the shop. Woody ran back into the shop on his own.

Woody entered the store just as it was about to close.

Woody picked up a pencil to defend himself, but Gabby Gabby didn't want
to harm Woody – she wanted him to understand her.

All Gabby Gabby wanted was a kid to love her. Woody made a decision.
He would give Gabby Gabby his voice box in exchange for Forky.

Gabby Gabby was delighted with her new voice box.
It worked perfectly!

Then, Woody heard Bonnie and her mum enter the shop.
He headed for the backpack, while Forky watched Gabby Gabby.
She had placed herself near Harmony. She pulled her string and
said, "I'm Gabby Gabby, and I love you."

But Harmony thought Gabby Gabby was too creepy.
She threw the doll into an old box!

Woody decided to go back and help Gabby Gabby. He told Forky to get Buzz to bring the campervan to the carnival. Then, he hopped out of the backpack and returned to the shop.

Woody told Gabby Gabby that Harmony wasn't her only chance at getting a kid – he would take her to Bonnie! "You can't sit on a shelf waiting for life to happen."

Unknown to Woody, Bo and the toys had returned to the shop to help him.

They needed Duke to jump over the carnival and land on top of the game booth so they could reach the campervan in time. Duke doubted himself, but Bo and Woody kept encouraging the daredevil. At last, he was ready.

Seconds later, Duke launched himself off the Ferris wheel, sailing over the carnival with ease. All memories of his past failures faded away as he crashed his bike right on target.

The toys zipped across the string of flags that Duke had pulled behind him. Just then, Gabby Gabby noticed a girl crying. She was lost and all alone.

The toys helped Gabby Gabby get the girl's attention.

The girl picked up the doll and hugged her tight. With Gabby Gabby, the girl worked up the courage to ask a security guard for help. She carried her new doll as she looked for her parents. Gabby Gabby finally had a kid.

Woody, Bo and the others met up with Bonnie's toys at the campervan. Everyone was happy to see them, and Woody was even happier to see Bonnie reunited with Forky. He had done the job he'd set out to do. It was then he realised that there were kids and toys everywhere who would always need his help.

Woody enjoyed helping kids and toys. And he knew that
wherever he went and whichever toy he helped next,
he would always have his friends by his side.